For DEAR LANABANANA

who dislikes the LIMELIGHT but looks VERY lovely in it.

LARRY ONLY deals with THE BEST

tiger tales
an imprint of ME Media, LLC

send LARRY FAN MAIL HERE please

202 Old Ridgefield Road
Wilton, CT 06897

Published in the United States 2011

Text and illustrations
© 2010 Leigh Hodgkinson

Limelight LARRY actually

Originally published in Great Britain 2010
by Orchard Books
a division of Hachette Children's Books,
a Hachette UK company (which IS a division of ...um... LIMELIGHT LTD)

CIP data is available

ISBN-13: 978-1-58925-102-1

ISBN-10: 1-58925-102-4

Printed in China

WKT 1010

YAWN BORING YAWN

so THIS Bit MEANS LARRY has THE copyright, right?

OR MORE IMPORTANTLY, LimeLight

For more insight and activities,
visit us at www.tigertalesbooks.com

LARRY

I ♡ LARRY

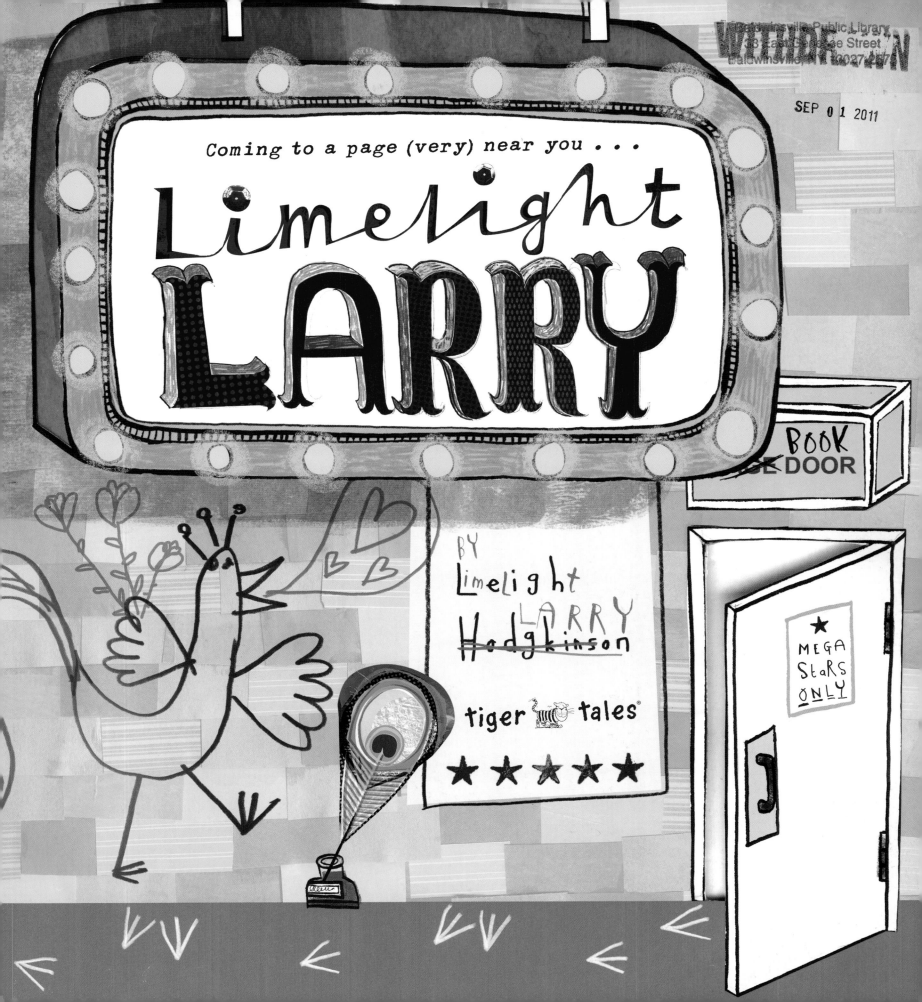

This is

Limelight

LARRY.

This is a book about him.

He thinks it will be an

AMAZING

book just because it
has him in it.

He thinks he is

the bee's knees with a cherry on top.

He thinks he should be

and that there should be
more books about him.

(Perhaps he should wait and see
if this book is any good first, huh?)

SUDDENLY

Limelight Larry spots something
out of the corner of his eye. . . .

"What do you want, Mouse?"
says Larry to *Mouse*.
"This is a book all about

ME, not .

There is NO room for you
on that page.

LOOK! You're making it all

messY!"

"Ooooh!" whispers *Mouse*.
"Is this a book, then?
Does this mean I'm in a
real live book?"

"Did I hear someone say this is a book?" says Bird,
who has appeared out of nowhere. "Can I be in it?
I could do something funny on the next page,
like hop on one leg for a bit or something."

"For your information, YES, this is a book," says Larry.

"But if <u>ANYBODY</u> is going to do anything funny, or even *slightly* amusing,

it will be

ME!

LARRY is not too keen on Bird (or anyone) stealing his limelight.

(This book is not called *Limelight Larry* for nothing, you know.)

It seems that **Elephant** was just in the neighborhood and has popped by to see what all the fuss is about.

Mouse tells him EVERYthing he knows about Larry's book (which isn't much).

HOP hOPPITY hOP hOP

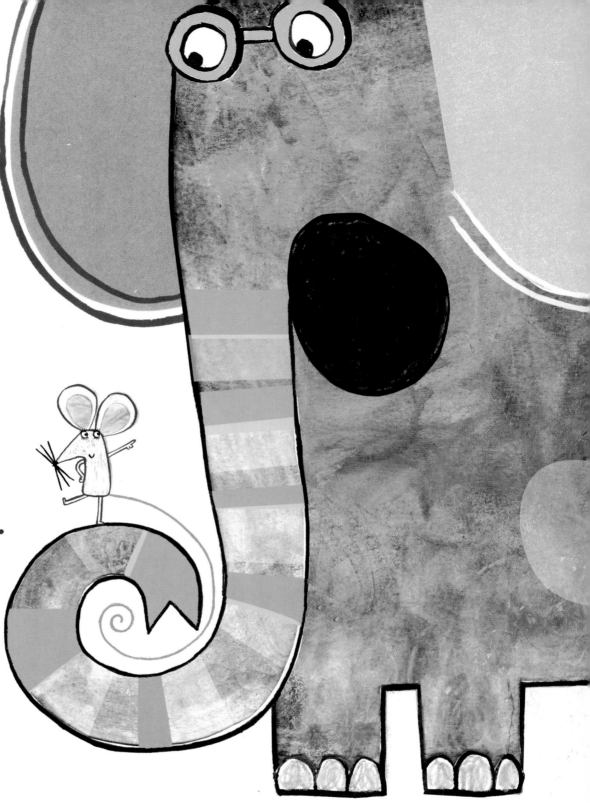

"In **MY** opinion," booms **Elephant**,

"the thing that makes a book interesting is a BIG surprise at the end."

"Maybe Elephant is the

BIG

surprise,"

suggests *Mouse* helpfully.

LARRY isn't the type of peacock who makes a habit of listening to the opinions of mice OR elephants. He secretly decides there will be no BIG surprises in THIS book. Besides, it's not anywhere near the end yet.

"Elephant's got a point, Larry," says *Wolf* (who must have been eavesdropping from over the page).

"But if you ask me . . .
what every fairy tale needs is a good
old-fashioned SCARY forest. It must be your
lucky day as I found this one out back!"

SNORT!

"Ooh, how very kind of
Wolf," squeals *Mouse*.

LARRY doesn't think so. Larry also doesn't think
the forest is in the least bit scary.
In fact, Larry thinks it's an AWFUL forest.

And, by the way, this book is certainly **NOT** a fairy tale.

With his snooty beak firmly up in the air, **LARRY** doesn't even notice that **Bear** has arrived.

(Everybody knows that bears love woodland tea parties.)

Bear looks at his watch. He is hoping that the other tea party guests won't be too late to be in the book.

Mouse
wonders if
there will be
cheesecake.

Wolf
hopes there will be a
Black Forest cake.

Bird
isn't really interested in
tea parties right now. . . .

Elephant worries there won't be enough Lemonade to go around . . .

while **LARRY** just CAN'T BELIEVE WHAT IS GOING ON!

This **whole** thing is getting **SILLY.**

The page is completely **cluttered**, and Larry's lovely feathers are starting to get all crimpled and crumpled.

This is **NOT** what he had hoped his book would be! Apart from there being

FAR far far FAR far FAR

too many words . . .

Bear is too popular,

Bunny is too cute,

Elephant is too big and smart,

Bird is too funny,

Wolf is too interested in fairy tales,

and *Mouse* is too nice and helpful (and has been in too many pages for Larry's liking).

It would be fair to say that

EVERYBODY

is cramping Larry's style!

SLURP

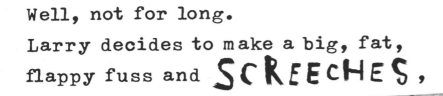
Well, not for long.
Larry decides to make a big, fat,
flappy fuss and SCREECHES,

"None of you NiTWiTS are even supposed to be here.
This is a Limelight LARRY book.
If you don't believe me, look on the cover!
So take the hint and GET LOST
and leave ME and my book ALONE!"

BUT it's far too late for that.
You see, everybody is ALREADY in the book.

Although, as far as Larry's concerned, it's definitely NOT too late. There is still one thing left to do . . .

take up the whole page himself and

SHOW OFF!

BUT
after a while . . .
Larry begins to wonder,
what is the point of showing off all by yourself?

It's CERTAINLY not much fun.

And,
oh dear,
the forest seems a lot more
SPOOKY and SCARY

now that Larry is all

ALONE and in the DARK.

Well, it looks as though
Elephant was right.

This book _does_ have a
BIG surprise at the end.

But who would have guessed the **BIG** surprise is . . .

Limelight LARRY
happily sharing the very LAST

and most <u>IMPORTANT</u> page with EVERYONE!

(Well, perhaps not the VERY last page.)

"**THanKS** for reading **MY** book **BUT**

Shhhhhh...

don't read it so loudly.

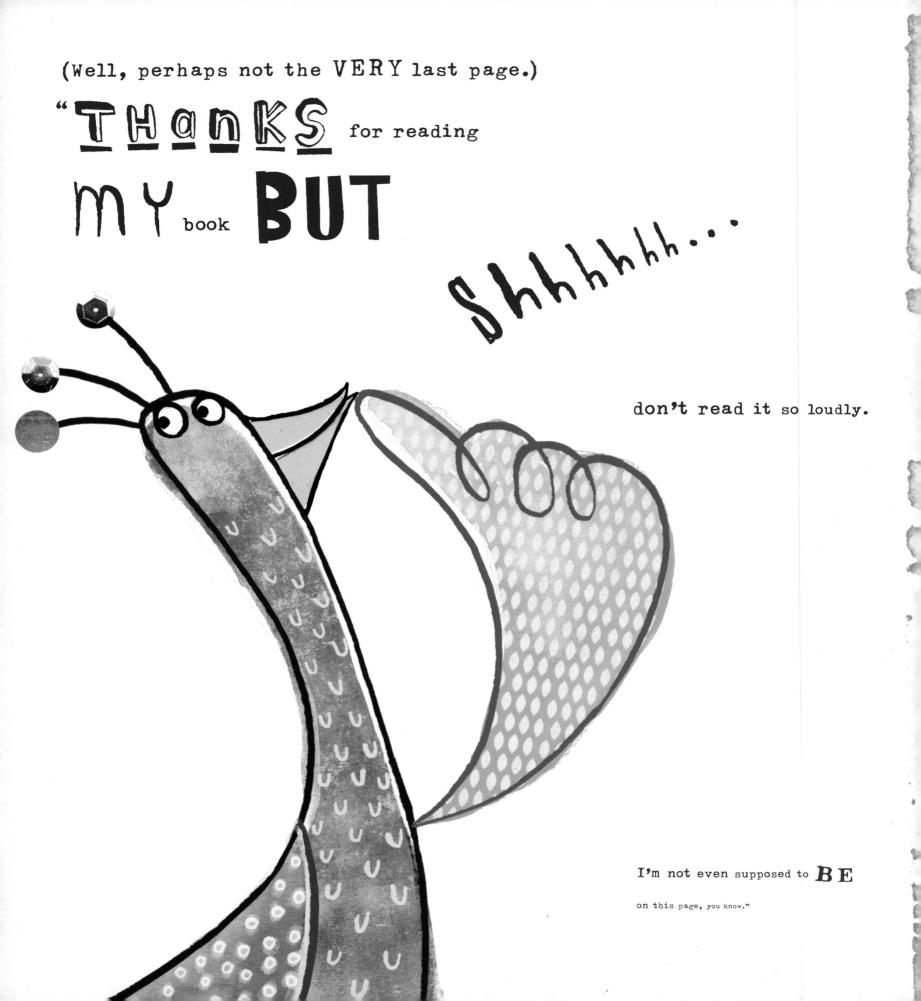

I'm not even supposed to **BE**

on this page, you know."